Dear Reader,

We're very pleased to present you with this gift.

Too Many Books! is the story of a boy named Nicholas who thinks there are far too many books in his life telling him *what to do* and *how to do* things. As you'll discover, Nicholas learns there are lots of different types of books available and the books he finds in his library really make him laugh!

At TD our employees are really excited to give you and every Grade One student in Canada a copy of *Too Many Books!* It's our way of celebrating TD Canadian Children's Book Week, one of the several children's reading programs we support each year across Canada. We encourage you to visit your local library to discover the magical world of books.

Have fun reading!

Ed Clark
President and CEO
TD Bank Financial Group

To Linda Clermont, lover of books
— G.T.

To my big-hearted father
— B. St-A.

Text copyright © 2003 by Gilles Tibo
Illustrations copyright © 2003 by Bruno St-Aubin
English text copyright © 2004 by Scholastic Canada Ltd.

Special edition prepared for the TD Grade One Book Giveaway Program.

This edition is published by special arrangement with the Canadian Children's Book Centre and TD Bank Financial Group
for free distribution to Grade One children across Canada during TD Canadian Children's Book Week 2008.

Scholastic Canada Ltd.
604 King Street West
Toronto, Ontario M5V 1E1
www.scholastic.ca

The Canadian Children's Book Centre
40 Orchard View Blvd., Suite 101
Toronto, Ontario M4R 1B9
www.bookcentre.ca

Printed and bound in Canada by Friesens Corporation.
Also available in French: *Des livres pour Nicolas!*

ISBN (English) 978-0-929095-46-2
ISBN (French) 978-0-929095-48-6

Library and Archives Canada Cataloguing in Publication

Tibo, Gilles, 1951-
[Des livres pour Nicolas!. English]
Too many books! / written by Gilles Tibo ; illustrated by Bruno
St-Aubin ; translated by Petra Johannson.

Originally publ.: Markham, Ont. : Scholastic Canada, 2004.
Edition financed by TD Bank Financial Group and distributed free to Canadian Grade One students
during TD Canadian Children's Book Week 2008.
ISBN 978-0-929095-46-2

I. St-Aubin, Bruno II. Johannson, Petra III. Canadian Children's
Book Centre IV. Title.
PS8589.I26D4813 2008   jC843'.54   C2008-902804-X

Mixed Sources
Product group from well-managed
forests and other controlled sources
www.fsc.org Cert no. SW-COC-1271
© 1996 Forest Stewardship Council
FSC

Too Many Books!

Written by Gilles Tibo

Illustrated by Bruno St-Aubin

The Canadian Children's Book Centre

One morning, Nicholas got dressed in a hurry and ran downstairs to find his mom. She gave him a hug, took one look at his shoelaces and said, "Nicholas, I have something for you."

Then she searched through a box and handed him a book about how to tie shoelaces.

4

After Nicholas read it, he could tie the best bows in the world.

When he finished his breakfast, he brushed his teeth very fast

VVVRRRiiiOOOUUUMMM!

Toothpaste flew all over the bathroom.

His dad ran in, gave him a kiss, and handed him another book – on how to brush your teeth.

BLUB! BLUB! BLUB!

After Nicholas read it, he had the whitest, brightest teeth in the world.

9

Then he tried to give his cat a bath. She did not want one.

His sister appeared, holding a book in her hands. Oh no! Not a book about how to wash cats!

11

After Nicholas read it, his cat was the cleanest, most beautiful cat in the world.

Nicholas decided to go outside and play. He tried riding his bike. It wasn't easy.

His favourite neighbour, Veronica, came over with a book under her arm.

"No!" said Nicholas. "You must be kidding! Not a book about how to ride like a pro!"

After Nicholas read it, he was the best bike rider in the world.

To thank Veronica, Nicholas went to the library with her. The minute they got there, she dove straight for the shelves and chose a stack of books.

Hugging her pile, she asked Nicholas, "Aren't you getting any?"

"No!" said Nicholas. "I'm tired of reading books that tell me how to do this, how to do that...how not to do this, how not to do that..."

Veronica grabbed him by the hand. "Look, Nicholas! Over here are adventures. Over there you'll find history. And down this row are the funny books."

To make her happy, Nicholas chose three – a pirate adventure, a book about knights and a funny story.

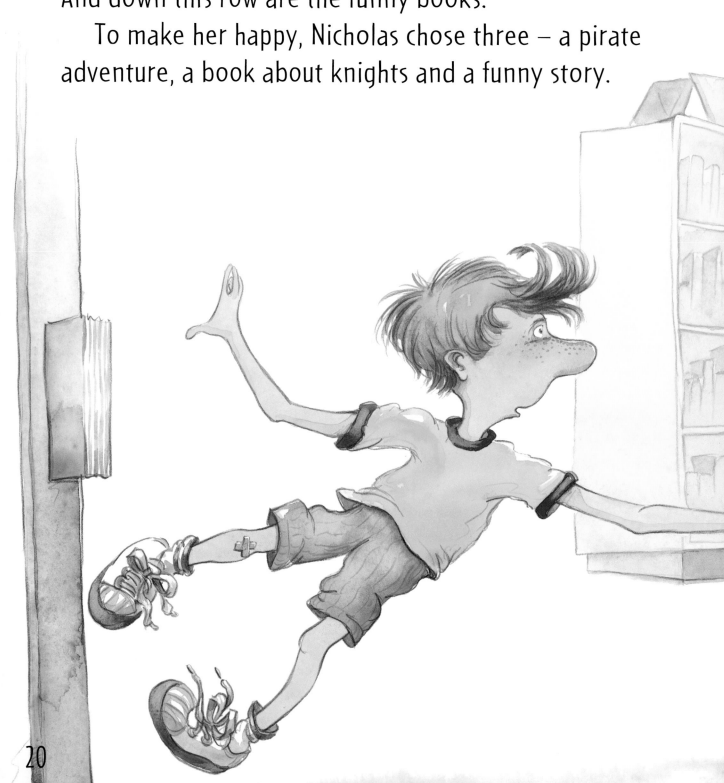

21

On the way back, Veronica kept saying, "I can't wait to read my books!"

"Um…uh…me, too…I can hardly wait…" said Nicholas.

At home, he headed to the backyard to play,
plunking his books on the grass. Hmm, he thought.
Should he give one of them a try?

Nicholas sat down under the tree, opened the funny book and started to read. He burst out laughing on the first page. And on the second page…
And the third…

He laughed so hard that his dad opened the back door and asked, "What's going on, Nicholas?"

His mom came out of the garage and asked,
"Nicholas, are you all right?"

Then his dad, his mom, his sister and Veronica all gathered around. With a big smile, Nicholas said, "Listen to this – 'Once there was a little mouse who…'"

After Nicholas finished, he was the happiest reader in the world!

Gilles Tibo

Gilles Tibo is known as much for his illustrations as for the stories that he writes. Since 1976 he has applied his creative talents to about a hundred books, including the popular Simon series. He has received top honours for his work, winning two Governor General's Awards and two Mr. Christie's Book Awards. He lives with his family in Montreal, Quebec.

Bruno St-Aubin

Bruno St-Aubin has been creating books for children since 1988. He has written and illustrated such books as *Daddy's a Dinosaur* and *My Favourite Monster*, and illustrated *Sadie the Ballerina* by Joan Betty Stuchner, *Where's My Hockey Sweater*, and *The Several Lives of Orphan Jack* by Sarah Ellis. He lives in Montreal, Quebec.

Dear Reader: Here are some other great Canadian children's books. The ones with a star ★ are suitable for readers ages 4 to 7.

2007 Award-Winning Canadian Children's Books

ALBERTA CHILDREN'S BOOK OF THE YEAR AWARD
Jamie Bastedo. *On Thin Ice*. Calgary: Red Deer Press, 2006.

ALCUIN SOCIETY AWARDS FOR EXCELLENCE IN BOOK DESIGN IN CANADA – Children's category
★ Chris Tougas. *Mechanimals*. Designers: Teresa Bubela and Chris Tougas. Victoria: Orca Book Publishers, 2007.

AMELIA FRANCES HOWARD-GIBBON ILLUSTRATOR'S AWARD
★ Mélanie Watt. *Scaredy Squirrel*. Toronto: Kids Can Press, 2006.

ANN CONNOR BRIMER AWARD FOR CHILDREN'S LITERATURE
Budge Wilson. *Friendships*. Toronto: Penguin Group (Canada), 2006.

ARTHUR ELLIS BEST JUVENILE CRIME AWARD
Seán Cullen. *Hamish X and the Cheese Pirates*. Toronto: Penguin Group (Canada), 2006.

BLUE SPRUCE AWARD
★ Mélanie Watt. *Scaredy Squirrel*. Toronto: Kids Can Press, 2006.

CANADIAN LIBRARY ASSOCIATION BOOK OF THE YEAR FOR CHILDREN AWARD
Hadley Dyer. *Johnny Kellock Died Today*. Toronto: HarperTrophyCanada, 2006.

CANADIAN LIBRARY ASSOCIATION YOUNG ADULT CANADIAN BOOK AWARD
William Bell. *The Blue Helmet*. Toronto: Doubleday Canada, 2006.

CHOCOLATE LILY YOUNG READERS' CHOICE AWARD
★ (Picture Book) Sarah N. Harvey. *Puppies on Board*. Illustrated by Rose Cowles. Victoria: Orca Book Publishers, 2005.
(Chapter Book/Novel) Polly Horvath. *The Vacation*. Toronto: Groundwood Books, 2005.

CHRISTIE HARRIS ILLUSTRATED CHILDREN'S LITERATURE PRIZE
Maggie de Vries. *Tale of a Great White Fish: A Sturgeon Story*. Illustrated by Renné Benoit. Vancouver: Greystone Books, 2006.

DIAMOND WILLOW AWARD
Marty Chan. *The Mystery of the Graffiti Ghoul*. Saskatoon: Thistledown Press, 2006.

ELIZABETH MRAZIK-CLEAVER CANADIAN PICTURE BOOK AWARD
Stéphane Jorisch. *The Owl and the Pussycat* by Edward Lear. Toronto: Kids Can Press, 2006.

GEOFFREY BILSON AWARD FOR HISTORICAL FICTION FOR YOUNG PEOPLE
Eva Wiseman. *Kanada*. Toronto: Tundra Books, 2006.

GOLDEN EAGLE CHILDREN'S CHOICE BOOK AWARD

Marilyn Halvorson. *Blood Brothers*. Markham, ON: Fitzhenry & Whiteside, 2004.

GOLDEN OAK AWARD

Pamela Porter. *The Crazy Man*. Toronto: Groundwood Books, 2005.

GOVERNOR GENERAL'S LITERARY AWARDS

★ (Illustration) Duncan Weller. *The Boy from the Sun*. Vancouver: Simply Read Books, 2006.

(Text) Iain Lawrence. *Gemini Summer*. New York: Delacorte Press, 2006.

HACKMATACK CHILDREN'S CHOICE BOOK AWARD

(Fiction) Pamela Porter. *The Crazy Man*. Toronto: Groundwood Books, 2005.

(Non-Fiction) Elizabeth MacLeod. *Harry Houdini: A Magical Life*. Toronto: Kids Can Press, 2005.

INFORMATION BOOK AWARD

Jan Thornhill. *I Found a Dead Bird: The Kids' Guide to the Cycle of Life & Death*. Toronto: Maple Tree Press, 2006.

IODE BOOK AWARD, MUNICIPAL CHAPTER OF TORONTO

Elizabeth Quan. *Once Upon a Full Moon*. Toronto: Tundra Books, 2007.

LILLIAN SHEPHERD MEMORIAL AWARD FOR EXCELLENCE IN ILLUSTRATION

★ Brenda Jones. *Skunks for Breakfast* by Lesley Choyce. Halifax: Nimbus Publishing, 2006.

MANITOBA YOUNG READERS' CHOICE AWARD

Pamela Porter. *The Crazy Man*. Toronto: Groundwood Books, 2005.

MARILYN BAILLIE PICTURE BOOK AWARD

★ Sara O'Leary. *When You Were Small*. Illustrated by Julie Morstad. Vancouver: Simply Read Books, 2006.

McNALLY ROBINSON BOOK FOR YOUNG PEOPLE AWARD

★ (Children's) Colleen Sydor. *Raising a Little Stink*. Illustrated by Pascale Constantin. Toronto: Kids Can Press, 2006.

(Young Adult) Larry Verstraete. *Lost Treasures: True Stories of Discovery*. Toronto: Scholastic Canada, 2006.

NATIONAL CHAPTER OF CANADA IODE VIOLET DOWNEY BOOK AWARD

Eric Walters. *Shattered*. Toronto: Viking Canada, 2006.

NORMA FLECK AWARD FOR CANADIAN CHILDREN'S NON-FICTION

Jan Thornhill. *I Found a Dead Bird: The Kids' Guide to the Cycle of Life & Death*. Toronto: Maple Tree Press, 2006.

OTTAWA BOOK AWARD

Janet Lunn. *A Rebel's Daughter: The 1837 Rebellion Diary of Arabella Stevenson*. Toronto: Scholastic Canada, 2006.

RED CEDAR BOOK AWARD

(Fiction) Kenneth Oppel. *Airborn*. Toronto: HarperCollins Publishers, 2004.

(Non-Fiction) Trudee Romanek. *Aha! The Most Interesting Book You'll Ever Read About Intelligence*. Illustrated by Rose Cowles. Toronto: Kids Can Press, 2004.

RED MAPLE AWARD

(Fiction) Eric Walters. *We All Fall Down*. Toronto: Doubleday Canada, 2006.

(Non-Fiction) Andreas Schroeder. *Thieves!* Toronto: Annick Press, 2005.

ROCKY MOUNTAIN BOOK AWARD

Pamela Porter. *The Crazy Man*. Toronto: Groundwood Books, 2005.

THE R. ROSS ANNETT AWARD FOR CHILDREN'S LITERATURE

Dale Auger. *Mwâkwa Talks to the Loon: A Cree Story for Children*. Surrey, BC: Heritage House, 2006.

RUTH AND SYLVIA SCHWARTZ CHILDREN'S BOOK AWARD

★ (Picture Book) Mélanie Watt. *Scaredy Squirrel*. Toronto: Kids Can Press, 2006.

(YA-Middle Reader) Deborah Ellis. *I Am a Taxi*. Toronto: Groundwood Books, 2006.

SASKATCHEWAN BOOK AWARD

R.P. MacIntyre. *Feeding at Nine*. Saskatoon: Thistledown Press, 2006.

SCIENCE IN SOCIETY BOOK AWARD

★ (Children's) Aubrey Lang. *Baby Sea Turtle*. Photography by Wayne Lynch. Markham, ON: Fitzhenry & Whiteside, 2007

(Youth) Julie E. Czerneda (Editor). *Polaris: A Celebration of Polar Science*. Illustrated by Jean-Pierre Normand. Markham, ON: Fitzhenry & Whiteside, 2007.

SHEILA A. EGOFF CHILDREN'S LITERATURE PRIZE

Sarah Ellis. *Odd Man Out*. Toronto: Groundwood Books, 2006.

SHINING WILLOW AWARD

★ David Ward. *The Hockey Tree*. Illustrated by Brian Deines. Toronto: North Winds Press/Scholastic Canada, 2006.

SILVER BIRCH AWARD

(Express) Nancy Shouse. *Any Pet Will Do*. Victoria: Orca Book Publishers, 2005.

(Fiction) L.M. Falcone. *Walking with the Dead*. Toronto: Kids Can Press, 2006.

(Non-Fiction) Kathy Kacer. *Hiding Edith*. Toronto: Second Story Press, 2006.

SNOW WILLOW AWARD

Arthur Slade. *Megiddo's Shadow*. Toronto: HarperTrophyCanada, 2006.

STELLAR BOOK AWARD

Carrie Mac. *The Beckoners*. Victoria: Orca Book Publishers, 2004.

TIME TO READ: THE BRITISH COLUMBIA ACHIEVEMENT FOUNDATION AWARD FOR EARLY LITERACY

★ Linda Bailey. *Stanley's Party*. Illustrated by Bill Slavin. Toronto: Kids Can Press, 2003.

TD CANADIAN CHILDREN'S LITERATURE AWARD

(English-language) Sarah Ellis. *Odd Man Out*. Toronto: Groundwood Books, 2006.

WHITE PINE AWARD

Eric Walters. *Shattered*. Toronto: Viking Canada, 2006.